THIS JOURNAL BELONGS TO

....

THE MORE GRATEFUL I AM, THE MORE BEAUTY I SEE

by THE GENTLE NOTEBOOK

the gentle notebook

WANT A FREEBIE !?

Follow us on Instagram

@gentlenotebook

&

Email us at

thegentlenotebook@gmail.com

Title your email with our secret code "G909", let us know that you have followed us and we will send some extra SURPRISES your way!

We create our journals with love and great care.

Yet mistakes can always happen. For any issues with your journal, such as faulty binding, printing errors, or something else, please do not hesitate to contact us by sending us a DM/Inbox at Instagram @gentlenotebook

We will make sure you get a replacement copy immediately.

DESIGNED by The Gentle Notebook

I Am Confident, Grateful & Blessed : A Self-Exploration & Gratitude Journal for Kids
Copyright © The Gentle Notebook 2020 - All rights reserved.

- NOTES -

📅 **DATE** _____ / _____ / 20 _____

I AM GRATEFUL FOR

1. _____
2. _____
3. _____

3 POSITIVE WORDS TO DESCRIBE MYSELF - I AM

*	*	*

WHAT WAS THE BEST PART OF YOUR DAY
write or draw about it

I FEEL

😄 → 🙂 → 😐 → 🙁 → 😣

DRAW
YOUR OWN SUPERHERO!

what superpowers does he/she have?

DATE _____ / _____ / 20 _____

I AM GRATEFUL FOR

1. _____
2. _____
3. _____

WHAT DID I LEARN TODAY

_____
_____
_____

WHAT WAS THE BEST PART OF YOUR DAY

write or draw about it

I FEEL

Write down 3 goals you'd like to achieve in your life. Be as specific as possible.

~ My dream list ~

 DATE _____ / _____ / 20 ___

I AM GRATEFUL FOR

1. _____
2. _____
3. _____

3 POSITIVE WORDS TO DESCRIBE MYSELF - I AM

*	*	*

WHAT WAS THE BEST PART OF YOUR DAY
write or draw about it

I FEEL

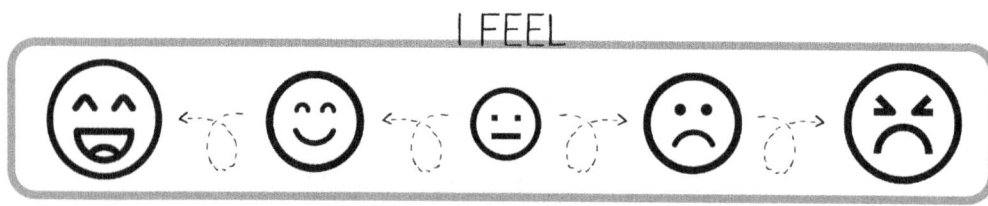

Write down 2 of the funniest things someone has said to you

SPREAD KINDNESS, SHARE THE LAUGHTER WITH SOMEONE TODAY BY SHARING YOUR FUNNIEST THINGS ON SOCIAL MEDIA WITH HASTAGS #Iamblessedgratitudejournal

📅 **DATE** _____ / _____ / 20 _____

I AM GRATEFUL FOR

1. _____
2. _____
3. _____

✨ WHAT DID I LEARN TODAY ✨

_____

_____

_____

WHAT WAS THE BEST PART OF YOUR DAY

write or draw about it

I FEEL

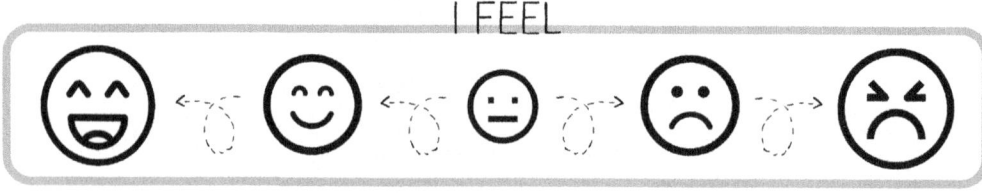

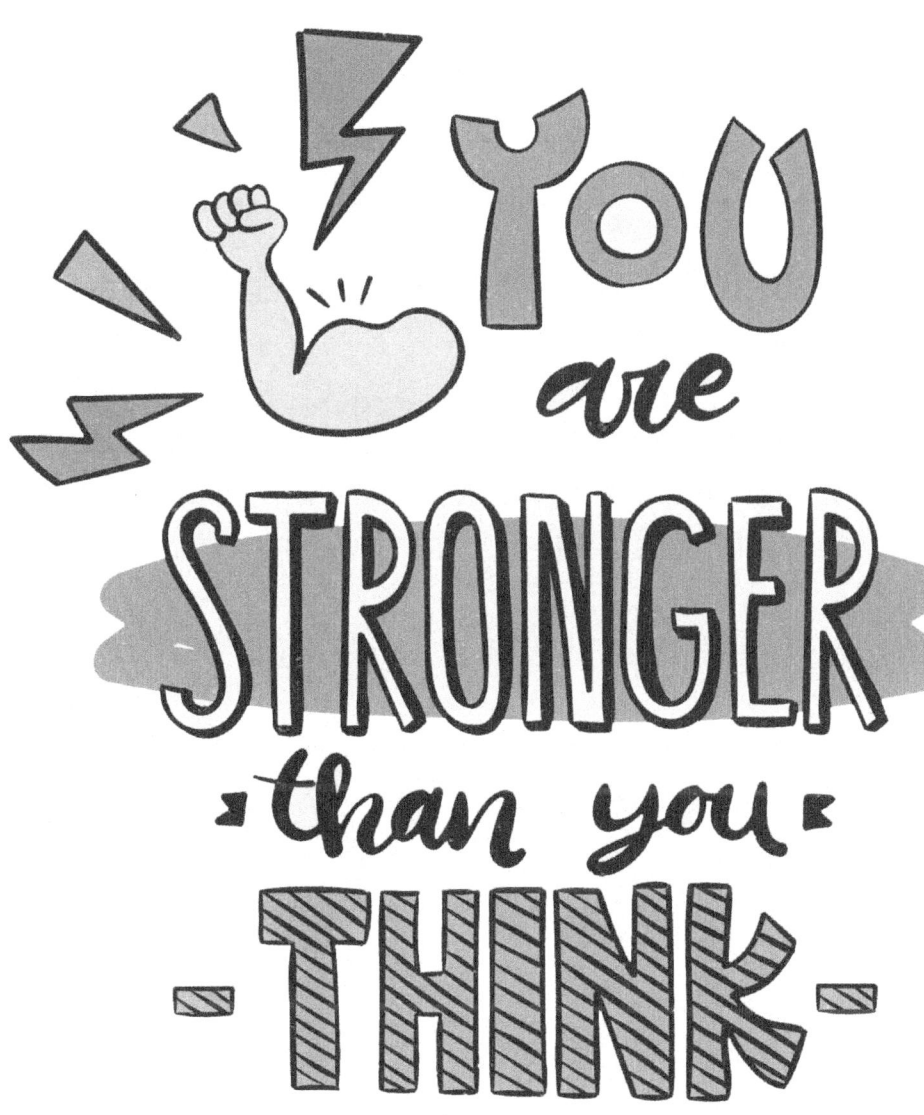

📅 **DATE** _____ / _____ / 20___

I AM GRATEFUL FOR

1. _____
2. _____
3. _____

3 POSITIVE WORDS TO DESCRIBE MYSELF - I AM

*	*	*

WHAT WAS THE BEST PART OF YOUR DAY
write or draw about it

I FEEL

Color the things you are grateful for

FRIENDS

FAMILY   PET   PENCIL

TEACHER   WEATHER

BAG

NEIGHBORS

WATCH   ARMS AND LEGS

SISTER   BROTHER

WATER   HOME

DATE _____ / _____ / 20 ___

I AM GRATEFUL FOR

1. _____
2. _____
3. _____

✨ WHAT DID I LEARN TODAY ✨

_____
_____
_____

WHAT WAS THE BEST PART OF YOUR DAY

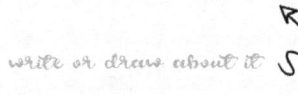

write or draw about it

I FEEL

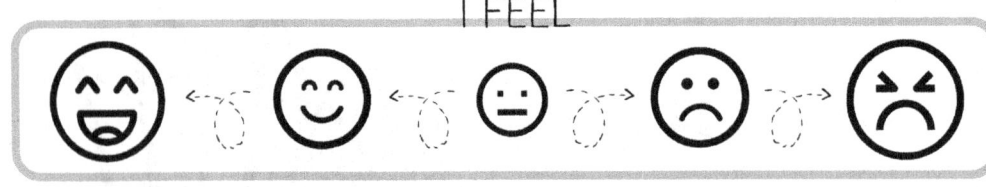

Write down 3 things you like about your body & why you are grateful for them?

I stand in awe of my body - Henry David Thoreau

DATE ____ / ____ / 20 ____

I AM GRATEFUL FOR

1. _____
2. _____
3. _____

3 POSITIVE WORDS TO DESCRIBE MYSELF - I AM

*	*	*

WHAT WAS THE BEST PART OF YOUR DAY

write or draw about it

I FEEL

GRATITUDE CHALLENGE

Tell two people about how grateful you are to

~ have them ~

DATE ____ / ____ / 20 ____

I AM GRATEFUL FOR

1. _____
2. _____
3. _____

WHAT DID I LEARN TODAY

_____
_____
_____

WHAT WAS THE BEST PART OF YOUR DAY

write or draw about it

I FEEL

😄 → 🙂 → 😐 → 🙁 → 😣

📅 **DATE** _____ / _____ / 20_____

I AM GRATEFUL FOR

1. _____
2. _____
3. _____

3 POSITIVE WORDS TO DESCRIBE MYSELF - I AM

*	*	*

WHAT WAS THE BEST PART OF YOUR DAY
write or draw about it

I FEEL

😄 → 🙂 → 😐 → 🙁 → 😫

LIST 5 THINGS THAT YOU HAVE
ACHIEVED AGAINST
ALL ODDS...

MY SUCCESS LIST

Always remember them and remind yourself when life gets hard

DATE ____ / ____ / 20 ____

I AM GRATEFUL FOR

1. _____
2. _____
3. _____

WHAT DID I LEARN TODAY

_____

_____

_____

WHAT WAS THE BEST PART OF YOUR DAY

write or draw about it

I FEEL

DATE _____ / _____ / 20_____

I AM GRATEFUL FOR

1. _____
2. _____
3. _____

3 POSITIVE WORDS TO DESCRIBE MYSELF - I AM

*	*	*

WHAT WAS THE BEST PART OF YOUR DAY
write or draw about it

I FEEL

DATE ____ / ____ / 20 ____

I AM GRATEFUL FOR

1. _____
2. _____
3. _____

WHAT DID I LEARN TODAY

_____
_____
_____

WHAT WAS THE BEST PART OF YOUR DAY

write or draw about it

I FEEL

📅 **DATE** _____ / _____ / 20 _____

I AM GRATEFUL FOR

1. _____
2. _____
3. _____

3 POSITIVE WORDS TO DESCRIBE MYSELF - I AM

*	*	*

WHAT WAS THE BEST PART OF YOUR DAY
write or draw about it

I FEEL

😄 → 🙂 → 😐 → 🙁 → 😖

Scribble your heart out

dump your stress, anger and fear with crayons and markers

📅 **DATE** _____ / _____ / 20 ___

I AM GRATEFUL FOR

1. _____
2. _____
3. _____

✨ WHAT DID I LEARN TODAY ✨

_____
_____
_____

WHAT WAS THE BEST PART OF YOUR DAY

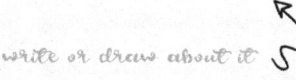
write or draw about it

I FEEL

List 3 things or activities you enjoy doing...

📅 **DATE** ____ / ____ / 20 ___

I AM GRATEFUL FOR

1. _____
2. _____
3. _____

3 POSITIVE WORDS TO DESCRIBE MYSELF - I AM

*	*	*

WHAT WAS THE BEST PART OF YOUR DAY
write or draw about it

I FEEL

😄 → 🙂 → 😐 → 🙁 → 😠

List down those who have hurt or angered you.

What will you do to forgive them?
*optional

Forgiveness is a form of
GRATITUDE

DATE ____ / ____ / 20 ____

I AM GRATEFUL FOR

1. _____
2. _____
3. _____

✨ WHAT DID I LEARN TODAY ✨

_____
_____
_____

WHAT WAS THE BEST PART OF YOUR DAY

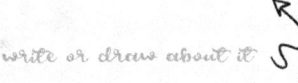
write or draw about it

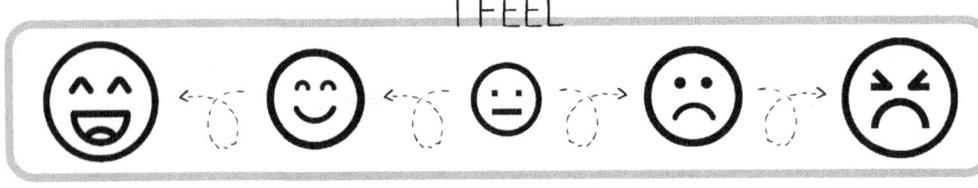
I FEEL

 DATE ____ / ____ / 20 ___

I AM GRATEFUL FOR

1. _____
2. _____
3. _____

3 POSITIVE WORDS TO DESCRIBE MYSELF - I AM

*	*	*

WHAT WAS THE BEST PART OF YOUR DAY
write or draw about it

I FEEL

GRATITUDE CHALLENGE
~ write a thank you note to someone ~

📅 **DATE** _____ / _____ / 20 ___

I AM GRATEFUL FOR

1. _____
2. _____
3. _____

✨ WHAT DID I LEARN TODAY ✨

_____
_____
_____

WHAT WAS THE BEST PART OF YOUR DAY

write or draw about it ↗

I FEEL

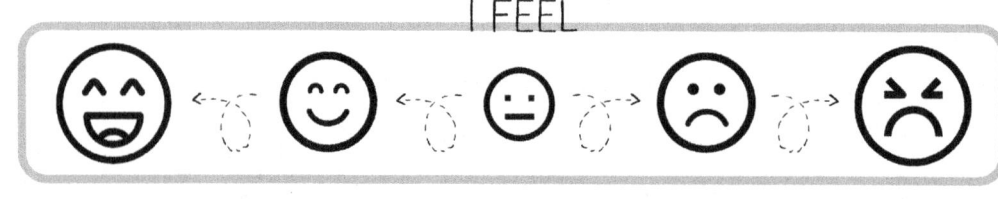

What is the most important lesson you've learned in life?

WHY?

INSPIRE OTHERS BY SHARING YOUR LESSON ON SOCIAL MEDIA WITH HASTAGS #Iamblessedgratitudejournal

📅 **DATE** ____ / ____ / 20 ___

I AM GRATEFUL FOR

1. _____
2. _____
3. _____

3 POSITIVE WORDS TO DESCRIBE MYSELF - I AM

*	*	*

WHAT WAS THE BEST PART OF YOUR DAY
write or draw about it

I FEEL

😄 → 🙂 → 😐 → 🙁 → 😖

Random Acts of Kindness

KINDNESS
IT COSTS NOTHING, BUT MEANS EVERYTHING

DATE ____ / ____ / 20 ____

I AM GRATEFUL FOR

1. _____
2. _____
3. _____

WHAT DID I LEARN TODAY

_____
_____
_____

WHAT WAS THE BEST PART OF YOUR DAY

write or draw about it

I FEEL

SAY THANKS, JUST THANKS TO YOUR PARENTS OR A PERSON FOR NO PARTICULAR REASON.

*

DESCRIBE THE PROCESS, YOUR FEELINGS, AND THOUGHTS *optional*

On a scale of 1-10, how hard was it?

1 easiest 2 3 4 5 6 7 8 9 10 hardest

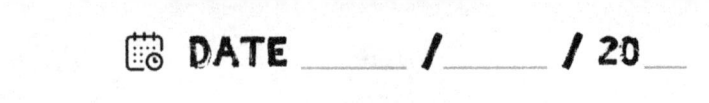

DATE _____ / _____ / 20___

I AM GRATEFUL FOR

1. _____
2. _____
3. _____

3 POSITIVE WORDS TO DESCRIBE MYSELF - I AM

*	*	*

WHAT WAS THE BEST PART OF YOUR DAY
write or draw about it

I FEEL

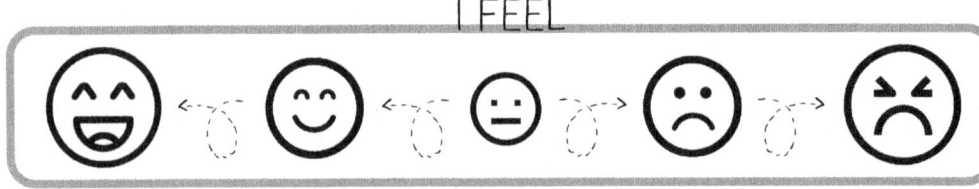

Day 2

LEAVE A KIND, FUNNY, OR INSPIRING NOTE IN A LIBRARY BOOK YOU'VE READ.

DESCRIBE THE PROCESS, YOUR FEELINGS, AND THOUGHTS *optional

On a scale of 1-10, how hard was it?

1 2 3 4 5 6 7 8 9 10
easiest   hardest

📅 **DATE** _____ / _____ / 20_____

I AM GRATEFUL FOR

1. _____
2. _____
3. _____

✨ WHAT DID I LEARN TODAY ✨

_____
_____
_____

WHAT WAS THE BEST PART OF YOUR DAY

write or draw about it

I FEEL

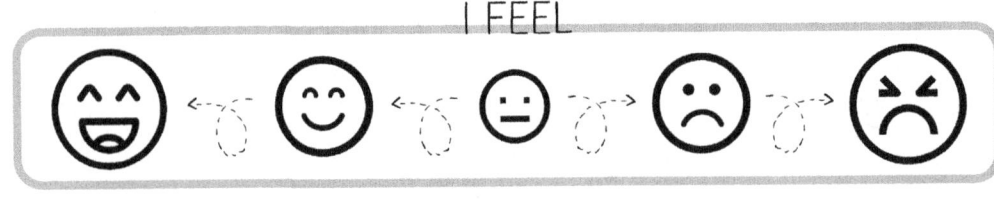

Day 3

DELIVER A COMPLIMENT TODAY—AND MEAN IT. DELIVER TWO IF YOU SEE IT MAKES FRIENDS AND FAMILY HAPPY.

DESCRIBE THE PROCESS, YOUR FEELINGS, AND THOUGHTS *optional

On a scale of 1-10, how hard was it?

1 easiest 2 3 4 5 6 7 8 9 10 hardest

📅 **DATE** _____ / _____ / 20___

I AM GRATEFUL FOR

1. _____
2. _____
3. _____

3 POSITIVE WORDS TO DESCRIBE MYSELF - I AM

*	*	*

WHAT WAS THE BEST PART OF YOUR DAY
write or draw about it

I FEEL

📅 **DATE** _____ / _____ / 20___

I AM GRATEFUL FOR

1. _____
2. _____
3. _____

✨ WHAT DID I LEARN TODAY ✨

_____
_____
_____

WHAT WAS THE BEST PART OF YOUR DAY

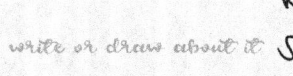
write or draw about it

I FEEL

Day 4

LEAVE A POSITIVE COMMENT OR WRITE A GLOWING REVIEW ON SOCIAL MEDIA

DESCRIBE THE PROCESS, YOUR FEELINGS, AND THOUGHTS *optional

On a scale of 1-10, how hard was it?

1 — easiest
2
3
4
5
6
7
8
9
10 — hardest

 **DATE** ____ / ____ / 20 ___

I AM GRATEFUL FOR

1. _____
2. _____
3. _____

3 POSITIVE WORDS TO DESCRIBE MYSELF - I AM

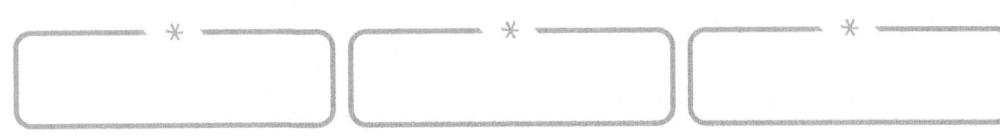

WHAT WAS THE BEST PART OF YOUR DAY
write or draw about it

I FEEL

Day 5

BE KIND TO A CLASSMATE YOU DON'T KNOW.

DESCRIBE THE PROCESS, YOUR FEELINGS, AND THOUGHTS *optional

On a scale of 1-10, how hard was it?

1   2   3   4   5   6   7   8   9   10
easiest   hardest

 **DATE** _____ / _____ / 20 ___

I AM GRATEFUL FOR

1. _____
2. _____
3. _____

✨ WHAT DID I LEARN TODAY ✨

_____
_____
_____

WHAT WAS THE BEST PART OF YOUR DAY

write or draw about it ↗

I FEEL

Day 6

DRAW A PICTURE ABOUT SOMETHING YOU LIKE ABOUT A PERSON & SEND IT TO HIM IN THE MAIL.

*

DESCRIBE THE PROCESS, YOUR FEELINGS, AND THOUGHTS *optional

On a scale of 1-10, how hard was it?

1 — easiest
2
3
4 ←
5
6 →
7
8
9
10 — hardest

DATE ___ / ___ / 20 ___

I AM GRATEFUL FOR

1. _____
2. _____
3. _____

3 POSITIVE WORDS TO DESCRIBE MYSELF - I AM

*	*	*

WHAT WAS THE BEST PART OF YOUR DAY
write or draw about it

I FEEL

Day 7

MAKE PEANUT BUTTER AND JELLY SANDWICHES FOR A LOCAL SHELTER.

GIVE

DESCRIBE THE PROCESS, YOUR FEELINGS, AND THOUGHTS *optional*

On a scale of 1-10, how hard was it?

1 easiest   2   3   4   5   6   7   8   9   10 hardest

DATE _____ / _____ / 20 _____

I AM GRATEFUL FOR

1. _____
2. _____
3. _____

✨ WHAT DID I LEARN TODAY ✨

_____
_____
_____

WHAT WAS THE BEST PART OF YOUR DAY

write or draw about it

I FEEL

😁 ← → 🙂 ← → 😐 ← → 🙁 ← → 😣

DATE _____ / _____ / 20 ___

I AM GRATEFUL FOR

1. _____
2. _____
3. _____

3 POSITIVE WORDS TO DESCRIBE MYSELF - I AM

*	*	*

WHAT WAS THE BEST PART OF YOUR DAY
write or draw about it

I FEEL

😁 ← 🙂 ← 😐 → ☹️ → 😠

WRITE DOWN 2 LITTLE THINGS THAT MADE YOU SMILE TODAY

 DATE _____ / _____ / 20 ___

I AM GRATEFUL FOR

1. _____
2. _____
3. _____

✹ WHAT DID I LEARN TODAY ✹

_____
_____
_____

WHAT WAS THE BEST PART OF YOUR DAY

write or draw about it ↰

I FEEL

List 2 talents you have.

how do you make use of them?

DATE ___ / ___ / 20___

I AM GRATEFUL FOR

1. _____
2. _____
3. _____

3 POSITIVE WORDS TO DESCRIBE MYSELF - I AM

| * | * | * |

WHAT WAS THE BEST PART OF YOUR DAY
write or draw about it

I FEEL

What is the Most AMAZING moment in your life!

DATE ____ / ____ / 20 ___

I AM GRATEFUL FOR

1. _____
2. _____
3. _____

WHAT DID I LEARN TODAY

_____
_____
_____

WHAT WAS THE BEST PART OF YOUR DAY

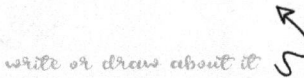
write or draw about it

I FEEL

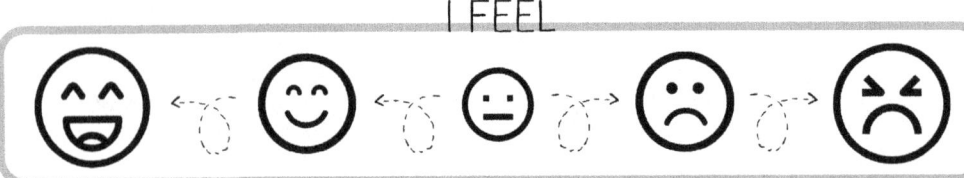

DATE ____ / ____ / 20 ____

I AM GRATEFUL FOR

1. _____
2. _____
3. _____

3 POSITIVE WORDS TO DESCRIBE MYSELF - I AM

*	*	*

WHAT WAS THE BEST PART OF YOUR DAY
write or draw about it

I FEEL

😁 ← 🙂 ← 😐 → ☹️ → 😣

~ List down all the people you love ~

To the world you may
be one person,
But to one person you
may be the world.
- Dr. Seuss

DATE _____ / _____ / 20 ___

I AM GRATEFUL FOR

1. _____
2. _____
3. _____

WHAT DID I LEARN TODAY

_____

_____

_____

WHAT WAS THE BEST PART OF YOUR DAY

write or draw about it

I FEEL

DRAW A PAST EVENT THAT YOU WILL WANT TO REMEMBER FOREVER

DATE _____ / _____ / 20 ___

I AM GRATEFUL FOR

1. _____
2. _____
3. _____

3 POSITIVE WORDS TO DESCRIBE MYSELF - I AM

* _____   * _____   * _____

WHAT WAS THE BEST PART OF YOUR DAY
write or draw about it

I FEEL

😁 → 🙂 → 😐 → 🙁 → 😣

What is your favorite movie and song?
WHY?

DATE ____ / ____ / 20 ___

I AM GRATEFUL FOR

1. _____
2. _____
3. _____

✨ WHAT DID I LEARN TODAY ✨

_____
_____
_____

WHAT WAS THE BEST PART OF YOUR DAY

write or draw about it

I FEEL

📅 **DATE** _____ / _____ / 20 _____

I AM GRATEFUL FOR

1. _____
2. _____
3. _____

3 POSITIVE WORDS TO DESCRIBE MYSELF - I AM

*	*	*

WHAT WAS THE BEST PART OF YOUR DAY
write or draw about it

I FEEL

Hey! You are Awesome

Glue in a photo of yourself that you dislike

Check every one of the boxes below to remind yourself how awesome you are. If you don't think the phrases are true, ask yourself why. Then, decide if you want to make changes (or not).

- ☐ I am loving
- ☐ I am beautiful
- ☐ I am strong
- ☐ I am amazing
- ☐ I am smart
- ☐ I am kind
- ☐ I am confident
- ☐ I am gifted
- ☐ I am blessed

- ☐ I am loved
- ☐ I am grateful
- ☐ I am thoughtful
- ☐ I am resilient
- ☐ I am exceptional
- ☐ I am _____
- ☐ I am _____
- ☐ I am _____
- ☐ I am discipline

📅 **DATE** _____ / _____ / 20 ___

I AM GRATEFUL FOR

1. _____
2. _____
3. _____

✨ WHAT DID I LEARN TODAY ✨

_____

_____

_____

WHAT WAS THE BEST PART OF YOUR DAY

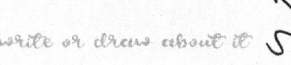
write or draw about it

I FEEL

What difficult situation are you grateful for...

We often take for granted the very things that most deserve our gratitude.
– Cynthia Ozick

📅 **DATE** _____ / _____ / 20 ___

I AM GRATEFUL FOR

1. _____
2. _____
3. _____

3 POSITIVE WORDS TO DESCRIBE MYSELF - I AM

*	*	*

WHAT WAS THE BEST PART OF YOUR DAY
write or draw about it

I FEEL

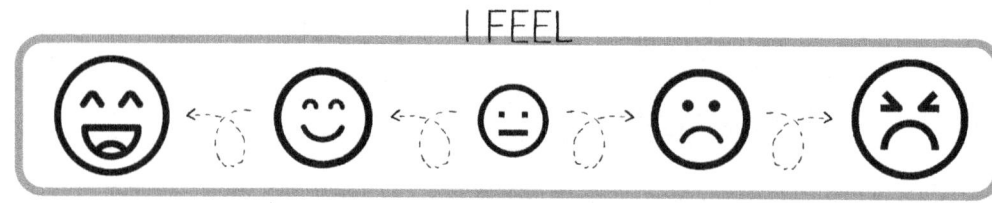

Write down three things that you APPRECIATE about your mom

"Feeling gratitude and not expressing it is like wrapping a present and not giving it."
~William Arthur Ward

📅 **DATE** ____ / ____ / 20 ____

I AM GRATEFUL FOR

1. _____
2. _____
3. _____

✸ WHAT DID I LEARN TODAY ✸

_____
_____
_____

WHAT WAS THE BEST PART OF YOUR DAY

write or draw about it ↱

I FEEL

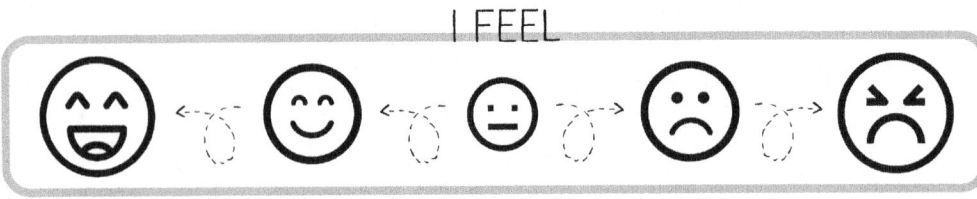

life is a gift

📅 **DATE** _____ / _____ / 20 ___

I AM GRATEFUL FOR

1. _____
2. _____
3. _____

3 POSITIVE WORDS TO DESCRIBE MYSELF - I AM

*	*	*

WHAT WAS THE BEST PART OF YOUR DAY
write or draw about it

I FEEL

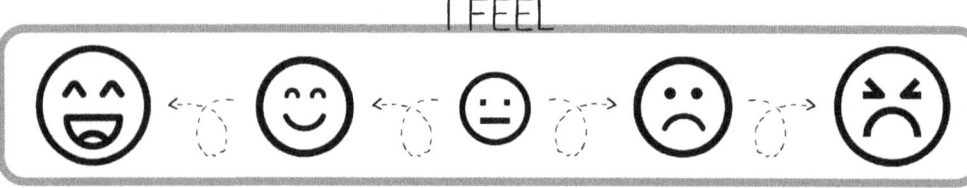

GRATITUDE CHALLENGE
24 Hours No Complaining Challenge

📅 **DATE** _____ / _____ / 20___

I AM GRATEFUL FOR

1. _____
2. _____
3. _____

✨ WHAT DID I LEARN TODAY ✨

_____
_____
_____

WHAT WAS THE BEST PART OF YOUR DAY

write or draw about it

I FEEL

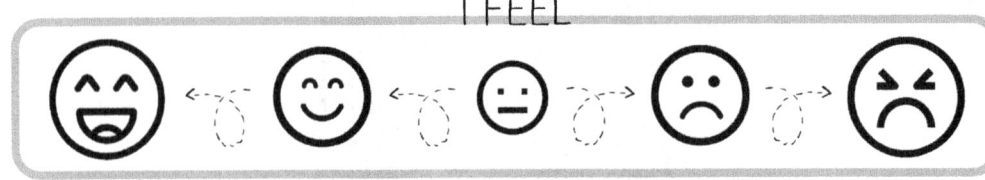

INSPIRE OTHERS BY SHARING YOUR STORY ON SOCIAL MEDIA WITH HASTAGS #Iamblessedgratitudejournal

Create your own comic

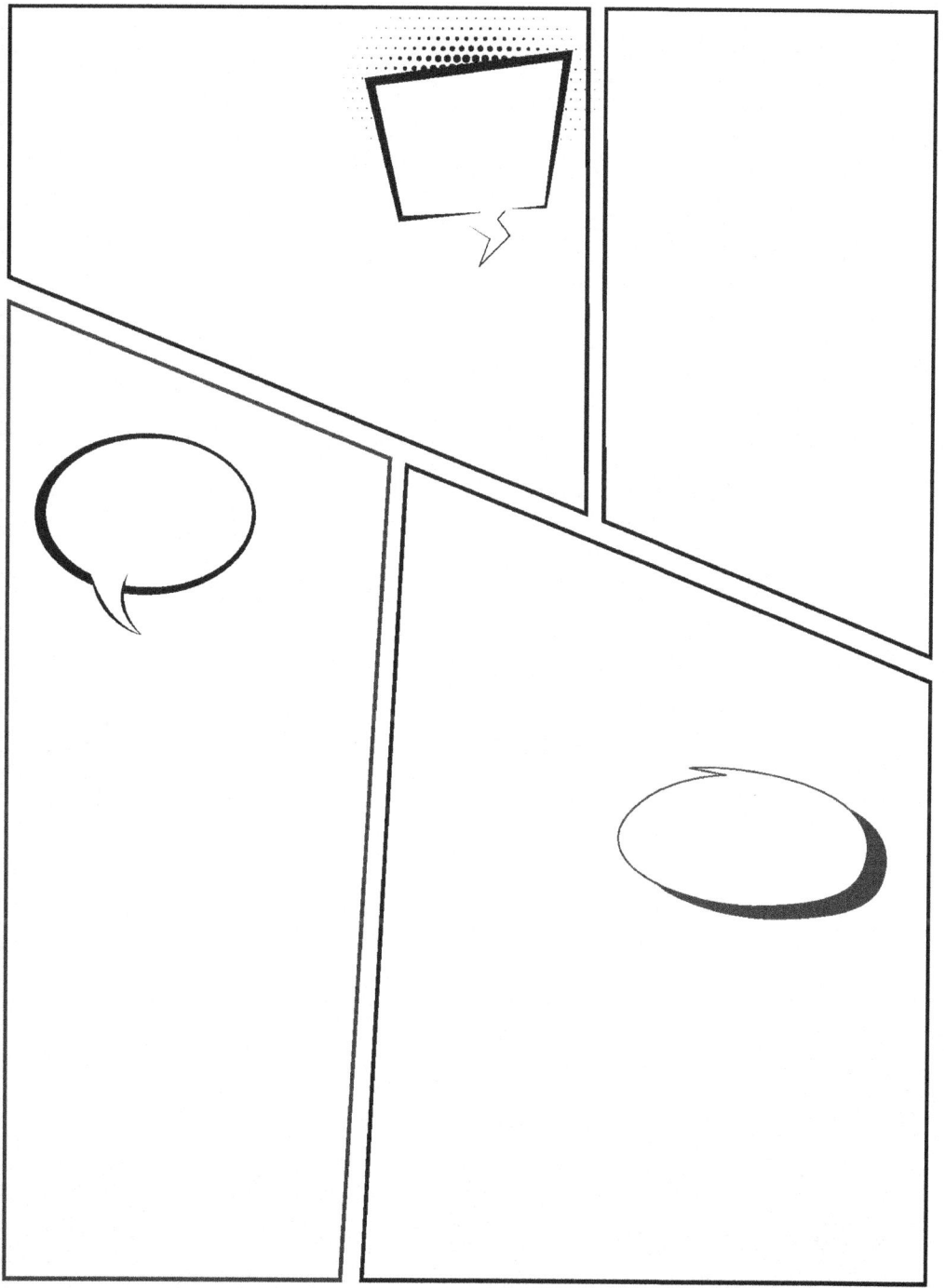

DATE _____ / _____ / 20 ___

I AM GRATEFUL FOR

1. _____
2. _____
3. _____

3 POSITIVE WORDS TO DESCRIBE MYSELF - I AM

*	*	*

WHAT WAS THE BEST PART OF YOUR DAY
write or draw about it

I FEEL

😄 → 🙂 → 😐 → 🙁 → 😣

DATE ____ / ____ / 20 ____

I AM GRATEFUL FOR

1. _____
2. _____
3. _____

WHAT DID I LEARN TODAY

_____
_____
_____

WHAT WAS THE BEST PART OF YOUR DAY

write or draw about it

I FEEL

📅 **DATE** _____ / _____ / 20 ___

I AM GRATEFUL FOR

1. _____
2. _____
3. _____

3 POSITIVE WORDS TO DESCRIBE MYSELF - I AM

*	*	*

WHAT WAS THE BEST PART OF YOUR DAY
write or draw about it

I FEEL

😁 → 🙂 → 😐 → 🙁 → 😣

What are the things that you desired so much, and you are having them now?

Be grateful for them

GRATITUDE
turns what we have into enough

📅 **DATE** _____ / _____ / 20 ___

I AM GRATEFUL FOR

1. _____
2. _____
3. _____

✨ WHAT DID I LEARN TODAY ✨

_____
_____
_____

WHAT WAS THE BEST PART OF YOUR DAY

write or draw about it

I FEEL

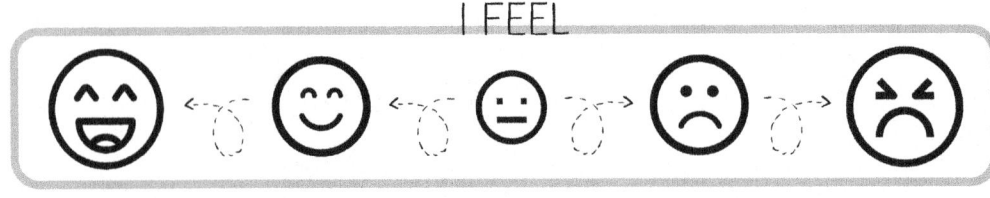

DATE _____ / _____ / 20 ___

I AM GRATEFUL FOR

1. _____
2. _____
3. _____

3 POSITIVE WORDS TO DESCRIBE MYSELF - I AM

*	*	*

WHAT WAS THE BEST PART OF YOUR DAY
write or draw about it

I FEEL

😄 → 🙂 → 😐 → 🙁 → 😣

WRITE DOWN THREE THINGS THAT YOU LIKE ABOUT SCHOOL
why?

DATE _____ / _____ / 20 ___

I AM GRATEFUL FOR

1. _____
2. _____
3. _____

WHAT DID I LEARN TODAY

_____
_____
_____

WHAT WAS THE BEST PART OF YOUR DAY

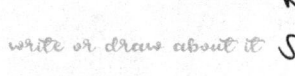
write or draw about it

I FEEL

5 Things I love about myself
write or draw

DATE _____ / _____ / 20 _____

I AM GRATEFUL FOR

1. _____
2. _____
3. _____

3 POSITIVE WORDS TO DESCRIBE MYSELF - I AM

*	*	*

WHAT WAS THE BEST PART OF YOUR DAY
write or draw about it

I FEEL

😁 → 🙂 → 😐 → 🙁 → 😣

Flood this page with good thoughts

IF YOU HAVE GOOD THOUGHTS, THEY WILL SHINE OUT
OF YOUR FACE A LIKE SUN BEAMS AND
YOU WILL ALWAYS LOOK LOVELY
~ROALD DAHL

- NOTES -

- NOTES -

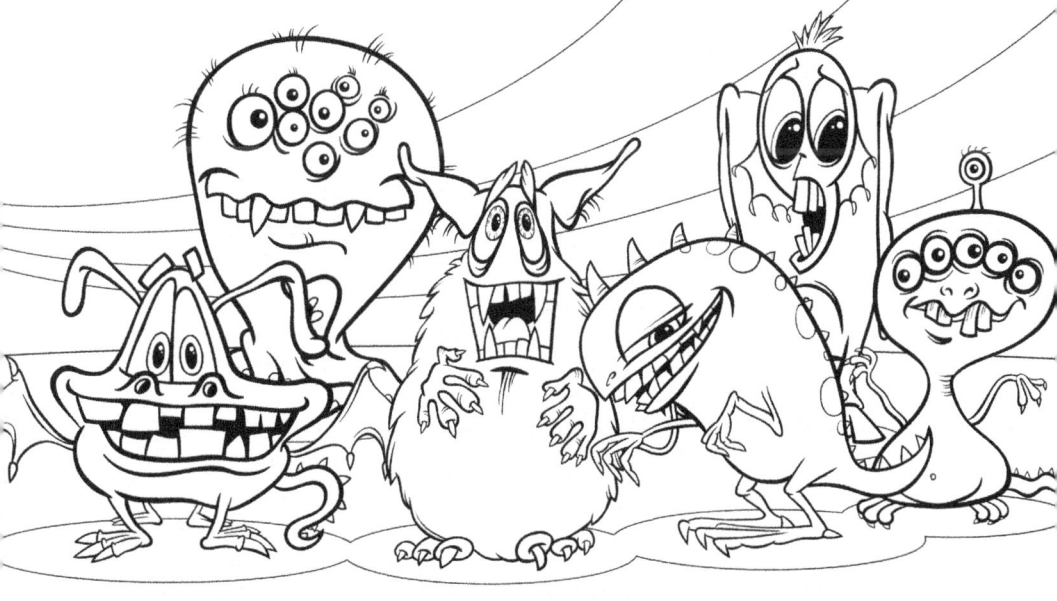

- NOTES -

My little Memory boxes

My little Memory boxes

also by
The Gentle Notebook
LOS ANGELES

~ Now Available! Check out our Instagram @gentlenotebook for more details ~

FOR ANY INQUIRIES OR QUESTIONS REGARDING OUR PRODUCTS, PLEASE CONTACT US AT thegentlenotebook@gmail.com

Made in the USA
Coppell, TX
25 March 2020